A Note to Parents and Caregivers:

Read-it! Readers are for children who are just starting on the amazing road to reading. These beautiful books support both the acquisition of reading skills and the love of books.

 The PURPLE LEVEL presents basic topics and objects using high frequency words and simple language patterns.

 The RED LEVEL presents familiar topics using common words and repeating sentence patterns.

 The BLUE LEVEL presents new ideas using a larger vocabulary and varied sentence structure.

 The YELLOW LEVEL presents more challenging ideas, a broad vocabulary, and wide variety in sentence structure.

 The GREEN LEVEL presents more complex ideas, an extended vocabulary range, and expanded language structures.

 The ORANGE LEVEL presents a wide range of ideas and concepts using challenging vocabulary and complex language structures.

When sharing a book with your child, read in short stretches, pausing often to talk about the pictures. Have your child turn the pages and point to the pictures and familiar words. And be sure to reread favorite stories or parts of stories.

There is no right or wrong way to share books with children. Find time to read with your child, and pass on the legacy of literacy.

Adria F. Klein, Ph.D.
Professor Emeritus
California State University
San Bernardino, California

Editor: Christianne Jones
Page Production: Joe Anderson
Creative Director: Keith Griffin
Editorial Director: Carol Jones
Managing Editor: Catherine Neitge
Editorial Consultant: Mary Lindeen
The illustrations in this book were done in watercolor.

Picture Window Books
5115 Excelsior Boulevard
Suite 232
Minneapolis, MN 55416
877-845-8392
www.picturewindowbooks.com

Printed in the United States of America.

Library of Congress Cataloging-in-Publication Data
Williams, Jacklyn.
Happy birthday, Gus! / by Jacklyn Williams ; illustrated by Doug Cushman.
p. cm. — (Read-it! readers)
Summary: Gus' Mom sends him to karate camp for his birthday, but Gus and Bean have
to put up with Billy when they get there.
ISBN-10: 1-4048-0957-0 (hardcover)
[1. Birthdays—Fiction. 2. Karate—Fiction. 3. Camps—Fiction. 4. Interpersonal
relations—Fiction. 5. Hedgehogs—Fiction.] I. Cushman, Doug, ill. II. Title. III. Series.

PZ7.W6656Ha 2005
[E]—dc22   2005003773

Happy Birthday, Gus!

by Jacklyn Williams
illustrated by Doug Cushman

Special thanks to our advisers for their expertise:

Adria F. Klein, Ph.D.
Professor Emeritus, California State University
San Bernardino, California

Susan Kesselring, M.A.
Literacy Educator
Rosemount–Apple Valley–Eagan (Minnesota) School District

PiCTURE WiNDOW BOOKS
Minneapolis, Minnesota

"I know your birthday isn't for a few days,"
Gus' mom said, "but I want you to open this
card today."

Gus opened the card and began to read.

Happy Birthday!
For an early birthday treat,
You are getting something neat,
It's not a bike
or a skateboard ramp —
I'm sending you to
Karate Camp!
Love, Mom

PS- Bean is going too

The next morning, Gus and Bean were at
the bus stop an hour early. They were really
excited for camp. When the bus finally
came, Gus thanked his mom for the
wonderful present. He gave her a kiss
goodbye, and then climbed on board.

6

As the bus pulled away from the curb, Gus waved goodbye.

"Have fun," called Gus' mom. "I'll see you in five days."

When they arrived at camp, Mr. Chase was
waiting for them. As they got off the bus, he
bowed. "Welcome," Mr. Chase said.

Billy stepped out from behind Mr. Chase.

"Yeah, welcome," Billy said in his nastiest voice. Gus looked at Bean and shook his head.

"It's going to be a long five days," Gus said.

Mr. Chase led them into the dining hall.
He bowed to them.

"At school, I am Principal Chase," he said.
"Here, I am Sensei Chase. Sensei means
teacher in Japanese."

10

Sensei Chase handed each of them a white uniform and a white belt.

"These are for you," he said. "The uniform is called a gi. The belt is an obi."

Sensei Chase clapped his hands.

"Before we begin our first karate class, each of you must make a pledge," he said.

"Raise your right hands, and repeat after me," he said.

"First, I promise to never use karate in anger. Second, I promise to use karate only when I am in class."

Everyone raised their right hands and repeated after Sensei Chase.

Just before Billy repeated the second part of the pledge, he slid his left hand behind his back. He crossed his fingers and lied about his promise.

After making the pledge, they practiced their moves. They kicked. They blocked. They punched the air. By the end of class, they were tired and sweaty.

Everyone picked up their things and
headed for the cabin area. "Don't forget
your pledge," said Sensei Chase.

"We won't," said Gus and Bean. Billy did
not say a word.

When they reached their cabin, they found three empty beds sitting side by side.

"Oh no," groaned Gus. "Billy is right next to us!"

Bean

Gus

Billy

Gus and Bean unloaded their backpacks and started unrolling their mattresses.

"That's not the way to make a bed," said Billy. "Let me show you how."

Billy raised his leg. "EEYAHHH!" he yelled.
Before Gus could remind him of his promise,
Billy gave the mattress a hard kick. The mattress
went flying. So did Billy. They landed in a heap
on the floor.

Early the next morning, Gus and Bean went
fishing before karate class.

"Catching fish with a pole is easy," said Billy.
"I'll show you the hard way."

As a big fish swam by, Billy raised his hand
and yelled "EEYAHHH!" The fish splashed,
and Billy screamed.

"You sure can't keep a promise, Billy,"
Bean said.

The following day the campers swam, hiked, and practiced karate. That night, Gus grabbed his flashlight and headed for the showers. The flashlight started blinking on and off.

"I think the batteries are going dead," said Gus.

Just then, Billy stepped out of the showers. "Here, let me help," he said. Billy karate-chopped the flashlight. The batteries popped out and hit him on the head.

"Ouch!" he cried, rubbing his head.

23

The final night of camp, the campers gathered around the campfire. Sensei Chase handed them each a stick with a marshmallow on the end of it. Billy grabbed Gus' stick.

"Your stick's longer than mine," he said. "I'll make it shorter."

"EEYAHHH!" yelled Billy.

CRACK went the stick. SPLAT went the marshmallow, right on Billy's chest. Gus just shook his head.

The following morning, Gus and Bean
packed up their gear. Gus sighed.

"Camp's over. By the time we get home, it'll
be too late for a birthday cake," he said.

Suddenly, a bell rang. "Oh boy, lunch!" said Bean. He rushed toward the dining hall.

Gus followed slowly behind.

When Gus walked into the dining hall, everyone yelled "SURPRISE!"

Gus looked around. There were balloons, streamers, and a huge chocolate cake.

"No cake or ice cream until you blow out the candles," said Sensei Chase. Gus took a deep breath. Before he could blow, Billy rushed over. "Let me help," he said.

"No," said Gus. "If you help, my wish won't come true."

Billy started punching the air, trying to create enough wind to blow out the candles.

"WATCH OUT!" shouted Gus. It was too late. Billy punched, and the cake squished. Billy dripped frosting, and Sensei Chase frowned.

"Do you think your wish will come true?"
asked Bean.

"I think it already did," said Gus.

"HAPPY BIRTHDAY, GUS!" yelled everyone.

More *Read-it!* Readers

Bright pictures and fun stories help you practice your reading skills. Look for more books at your level.

Happy Easter, Gus!
Happy Halloween, Gus!
Happy Thanksgiving, Gus!
Happy Valentine's Day, Gus!
Let's Go Fishing, Gus!
Make a New Friend, Gus!
Merry Christmas, Gus!
Pick a Pet, Gus!
Welcome to Third Grade, Gus!

Looking for a specific title or level? A complete list of *Read-it!* Readers is available on our Web site: **www.picturewindowbooks.com**